Milo

Imagines the World

TWO HOOTS

Written by
MATT DE LA PEÑA

Illustrated by
CHRISTIAN ROBINSON

What begins as a slow, distant glow
grows and grows
into a tired train that clatters down the tracks.
A cool rush of wind quiets into a screech of steel,
and when the doors slide open, Milo slips aboard.

MiLO

IMAGINES THE WORLD

The train bucks back into motion
as he and his sister squeeze onto bench seats.
The whiskered man beside Milo has a face of concentration.

The wedding-dressed woman near the far door
has a face made out of light,
while the dog peeking out of her handbag has no face at all

These monthly Sunday train rides
are never ending, and as usual, Milo is a shook-up soda.
Excitement stacked on top of worry
on top of confusion
on top of love.
To keep himself from bursting, he studies
the faces around him and makes pictures of their lives.

At a local stop, the whiskered man folds up
his crossword and hurries off the train.

Milo imagines him trudging
through brown mounds of slush.
It's a five-flight climb
to his cluttered apartment,
where he's greeted by mewling cats
and burrowing rats.

Parakeets tweet songs of longing
as the man sips tepid soup,
hunched over a game of solitaire.

Late that night,
the door to the parakeet cage
mysteriously falls open,
and the cats gather on the cold sill
to watch the birds fly free above the city.

Milo tugs his sister's sleeve and holds up his picture.
But even when she turns to look, he can tell she doesn't see.

A boy in a suit boards the train with his dad.
His hair is a perfect part, and there's not a single scuff
on his bright white Nikes.

Milo imagines the *clop clop clop*
of the horse-drawn carriage
that will carry him to his castle.

Imagines the *clink clink clink*
of the guards slowly lowering the drawbridge.

Across the human-made moat
the boy is met by a butler, two maids,
and a gourmet chef offering
crust-free sandwich squares.

Milo flips to a fresh page at a bustling city stop.
When the wedding-dressed woman strides off the train,
a band of street performers launches into "Here Comes the Bride,"
and everyone on the platform stops and cheers.

Milo imagines
the grand cathedral ceremony
where the couple will be pronounced
husband and wife.

Imagines the groom whisking his new bride
to an awaiting hot air balloon, where the pilot
loads them in with blankets and blasts the heat.
And up, up they go, hand in hand,
beyond the concrete walls of the city,
into the infinite blue.

Milo holds up this picture, too,
but his sister shoos him away.
"Can't you see I'm playing my game?"

He watches her thumbs
bang around her smudged screen,
then turns back to the boy in the suit.

They lock eyes for a few long seconds,
and suddenly it feels like the walls
are closing in around Milo.

The spell is broken when a crew of break dancers
bounds onto the train, announcing, "You all ready for a show?"
Several curious faces look up as the beat drops.
And now the girls are walking up walls,

they're whirling around poles,
they're backflipping over shopping bags.
When the train pulls into the next stop,
they collect a few coins and scramble to another carriage.

Milo imagines them going from train to train,
doing their act as everyone watches.

But even after the performances are over,
faces still follow their every move.
When they walk down
the electronics aisle
at the department store.

When they cross into the fancy neighbourhood.

Milo doesn't really like this picture,
so he puts away his pad and turns
to his reflection in the window.

What do people imagine
about *his* face?

Can they see him reciting
his volcano poem to the class?

Can they hear his mum's soothing voice
reading him a bedtime book
over the phone?

Can they smell the chile colorado
bubbling in a pot
in his auntie's apartment
near the cemetery?

Butterflies flood Milo's stomach
when it's finally their stop.
He follows his sister onto the cold station p
and up the stairs.

Above ground, he's surprised to see
the boy in the suit a few paces ahead.

He's even more surprised when the boy joins the long line
to pass through the metal detector.
Milo's sister suddenly bends to give him a hug.
"I didn't mean to snap at you," she says.
She takes his hand, adding, "You have your picture ready?"
He nods, feeling the warmth of her fingers.

As they slowly shuffle forward,
Milo studies the boy in the suit,
his dad rubbing his thin shoulders.
And a thought occurs to him:
Maybe you can't really know anyone
just by looking at their face.

Milo tries to reimagine all the pictures
he made on the train.
Maybe he could have done it like this instead.

Or this.

Or this.

Milo's chest fills with excitement
when he spots his mum through the crowd.

His sister rushes to give her a hug
before pulling Milo in, too.
And it's in this tight tangle of familiar arms
that he feels most alive.

When they separate, Milo flips through his pad
until he finds the right picture.
"I made this for you," he says, holding it up.
And he watches for the smile
he hopes will spread across his mum's face.

For Miguel de la Peña.
And for those who dare to imagine
beyond a first impression – M. de la P.

For the children, and inner children,
who see themselves in this book – C. R.

First published in the USA 2021 by G. P. Putnam's Sons
This edition published in the UK 2021 by Two Hoots
an imprint of Pan Macmillan
6 Briset Street London EC1M 5NR
Associated companies throughout the world
www.panmacmillan.com

ISBN 978-1-5290-6631-9

1 3 5 7 9 8 6 4 2

A CIP catalogue record for this book is available from the British Library.
Printed in Spain

Design by Eileen Savage

The illustrations in this book were created with acrylic paint, collage and a bit of digital manipulation.

www.twohootsbooks.com

READY to RIDE

For my brother Christophe, who was there when my little wheels were taken off.
Thanks to David, for the spark.
Thanks to Servane, Camille, Anne-Claire and Héloïse for their precious help.

sp

Q **QuartoKnows**

Quarto is the authority on a wide range of topics.

Quarto educates, entertains and enriches the lives of
our readers—enthusiasts and lovers of hands-on living.

www.quartoknows.com

© Flammarion 2017. Original edition "mes petites roues"
This edition © Quarto Publishing plc
Translated from the French by Vanessa Miéville

First published in the English language in 2018 by
words & pictures, an imprint of The Quarto Group.
The Old Brewery, 6 Blundell Street,
London N7 9BH, United Kingdom
T (0)20 7700 6700 F (0)20 7700 8066
www.QuartoKnows.com

British Library Cataloguing in Publication Data available on request

ISBN: 978-1-91027-772-0

1 3 5 7 9 8 6 4 2

Manufactured in Dongguan, China TL012018

FSC
www.fsc.org

MIX
Paper from
responsible sources
FSC® C104723